D0342477

# MONSTER HIGH™

SOPHIE FINN

Little, Brown and Company
New York Boston

This book is a work of fiction. Names, characters, places, and incidents are the product of the author's imagination or are used fictitiously. Any resemblance to actual events, locales, or persons, living or dead, is coincidental.

MONSTER HIGH and associated trademarks are owned by and used under license from Mattel. © 2018 Mattel. All Rights Reserved.

Cover design by Véronique L. Sweet. Cover illustration by Melissa Manwill.

Hachette Book Group supports the right to free expression and the value of copyright. The purpose of copyright is to encourage writers and artists to produce the creative works that enrich our culture.

The scanning, uploading, and distribution of this book without permission is a theft of the author's intellectual property. If you would like permission to use material from the book (other than for review purposes), please contact permissions@hbgusa.com. Thank you for your support of the author's rights.

Little, Brown and Company
Hachette Book Group
1290 Avenue of the Americas, New York, NY 10104
Visit us at LBYR.com
monsterhigh.com

First Edition: July 2018

Little, Brown and Company is a division of Hachette Book Group, Inc.
The Little, Brown name and logo are trademarks of Hachette Book Group, Inc.

The publisher is not responsible for websites (or their content) that are not owned by the publisher.

Library of Congress Control Number 2018932054

ISBN: 978-0-316-51267-1 (pbk.)

Printed in the United States of America

LSC-C

10 9 8 7 6 5 4 3 2 1

*To Brooke and Emily*

## CHAPTER 1

# Lights, Camera, Fashion!

"Oh my claws!" exclaims Pawla. The little ghoul holds up her hands. She is sitting in the Creepeteria working on a jewelry project, but she has just realized something terrible. Her claws are chipped. They are a mess!

Pawla likes to have perfectly painted fingers. She loves to look spooky and stylish—just like her older sister, Clawdeen. "I've been too busy making new friends to freshen up my full-moon polish," Pawla realizes.

Pawla is part of a big werewolf family. She has a big sister and lots and lots of brothers. She's happy that her werefamily lives in the Monster High castle. It's a great place to meet cool new ghouls and learn about other monsters. What Pawla loves best are all the spooktacular styles—from batwing backpacks to mummy-wrap leggings.

Pawla loves to fang out with her family, especially her rough-and-tumble brothers. But she also loves to do girly-ghoul things like painting her claws and making jewelry too.

*Clawdeen loves girly-ghoul activities too*, thinks Pawla. She hops up from her seat. She puts a final bead on the bracelet she is making. All done! "I'd better go find my big sister! Then we can paint our claws together."

Pawla heads into the howlway of Monster High. It is full of students hurrying to their coffin lockers. *I wish I were old enough to go to class and help out with Monster High activities*, thinks Pawla. She's still too young to be an official student. But she likes watching all her older sister's friends on their way to study. She daydreams about when she can finally join them.

*My favorite class would be Home Ick because you learn to sew and knit...* Pawla thinks as she peeks into a classroom.

The Monster High students look busy as they learn how to use a cobweb-thread sewing machine. But they also look like they're having a clawesome time.

*I'd also love art class...* Pawla decides

as she continues down the howlway. *Then I could make painted beads for my jewelry.*

The art room door is open, and something crazy is going on inside! Sparkles glitter in the air. Feathers waft into the howlway. Pawla watches a purple shape float past the door.

Is that a ghost? No! It's a piece of thin, shiny silk.

What is going on?

Pawla peers into the room. There is Clawdeen! She is humming to herself as she glues feathers and glitter onto a long, sparkly dress.

What fun! This is exactly what Pawla wants to be doing. Her sister is the best.

A feather lands on her nose. *Achoo!*

CHAPTER 2

# Project Runway

"Who's sneezing up a storm in here?" asks Clawdeen, looking up. She can't see through the cloud of sparkles and feathers.

"Hi, big sis!" Pawla calls out. "What are you doing?"

"Oh my claws!" exclaims Clawdeen. She pulls a feather covered in glue from her fingers. "I didn't see you come in, Pawla.

I'm creating some fabulous new fashions!" Clawdeen picks up her glue gun and sticks another feather onto the fabric. As she works, she sings a song:

*"It's so much better to have a sweater*
*as stylish and sweet as a Halloween treat!"*

"I love that song!" exclaims Pawla, recognizing Ari Hauntington's "Spooktastic Styles." It's one of Pawla's favorites because it's all about monster fashion. She likes to listen to it through her iCoffin headphones while she makes jewelry.

Her sister grins and the ghouls sing together:

*"I've got style and you've got*
*passion.*
*But together we can create*
*spooktastic fashion."*

"I wanted to see if we could fang out," Pawla tells Clawdeen when they finish singing. "I brought some full-moon claw polish. Want to paint our claws together?"

Clawdeen looks torn. She glances at her own claws. They *definitely* could use a fresh coat.

"I totally wish I had time," she apologizes. "I would love to fang out. But I'm rushing to finish this project. I'm putting on my very own fashion show!"

"A fashion show!" Pawla is delighted. "For what?"

Clawdeen smiles and stands up. She holds out her finished dress. It glitters and gleams. Perfect for a monster queen!

"Mom is putting on a Monster High art show. And every monster is doing something cool. There are going to be sculptures and videos and paintings," explains Clawdeen. She picks up an unfinished pair of mansterfriend jeans. They look too Normie. What will she glue onto them to make them more creeptastic? Can she add an artfully ripped hole to the knee?

Pawla does a little dance because she is so excited. This is going to be amazing. A fashion show! Her favorite. "I can't wait to get involved," she tells her sister. "I check out new styles all day long and I have so many ideas! Floral versus frightful patterns is the really big question. . . ."

"What's got my children so worked up?" comes a friendly voice from the doorway.

It's Mrs. Wolf, Clawdeen and Pawla's mom. Her arms are full of fabric and she's using a tape measure as a headband. There's a feather behind her ear and a long stream of ribbons dangling around her neck.

"Mom!" both wereghouls cry.

"You look so silly!" Pawla giggles.

"Silly *and* stylish," jokes Mrs. Wolf. "I was just bringing Clawdeen these supplies for her finishing touches."

"Thanks! I'm almost done!" Clawdeen eagerly takes the decorations from her mom and puts them into the coffin-shaped basket at her feet. "But this material will be useful. I still need to make a cape for Gilda Goldstag. It has to look just like a Golden Hind pelt."

“Mom! What can I do for the art show?” Pawla asks eagerly. She’s already bursting with ideas. What could she contribute to the show? *I could make a jewelry display or paint a series of claw-polish portraits.*

“Oh no.” Mrs. Wolf looks worried. She sighs.

“What is it?” Pawla asks.

“Well...” Mrs. Wolf wrings her hands. “I’m sorry, my dear. The art show is only for older Monster High students.”

“That’s too bad,” Clawdeen says, patting her little sister on the shoulder. “But that gives Pawla even more time to think of something extra spooky for *next* year’s art show.”

Pawla nods. She wants her mom’s art show to be a success—and she definitely doesn’t want to get in the way. Still, she can't hide her disappointment. It looks as if Clawdeen and Mrs. Wolf are super busy.

"Don't worry," Clawdeen reassures Pawla, seeing her frown. "We'll fang out soon enough. In the meantime, you should go find Barker. He definitely has some free time."

Pawla nods enthusiastically. Clawdeen is right. Barker is her brother *and* her best friend. Their favorite game to play together is Fetch. But maybe she can convince him to do some girly-ghoul things. Pawla doesn't have to be part of the art show to be creative. She can design jewelry and test out new hairstyles with Barker. Maybe he will even let her paint his claws!

"I'm lucky to have such a big family," she says out loud as she heads back into the howlway. "There's always someone who has time to play!"

## CHAPTER 3

# Stitch by Stitch

Pawla searches for her pack of brothers. They play so much hide-and-creep that they have discovered the secret spots all over the castle. Pawla sighs.... *They are always finding new places to get into trouble.*

Pawla notices that everywhere she goes, mansters and ghouls are working on spooktacular art projects. Everyone is getting ready for the show.

"Hey! What are you up to?" she asks Draculaura. The cool older ghoul is sitting in front of a computer in the Mad Science lab. Draculaura taps on the keyboard and a video clip appears on the screen. It's of Draculaura and her little sister, Fangelica, baking together.

Draculaura notices Pawla beside her. She pushes a strand of pink hair behind her ear. "Hi, Pawla!" She pauses the video. "I'm just editing my video for the art show."

"Cool! Can I see?" Pawla peers over her friend's shoulder. Draculaura is wearing dangling jewel bug earrings. Pawla makes a mental note. She'd love to bead some of those for her art project next year.

Draculaura laughs and shuts off the computer. "Definitely...but when it's finished. I want it to be really good!"

"Okay! Good luck!" Pawla says good-bye to her older sister's friend. She's excited to see Draculaura's video. But she understands wanting a project to be perfect.

On her way to the library, Pawla runs into Frankie. Frankie's arms are full of special glow-in-the-dark paint cans. There's paint on her hands, on her skirt, and even on her face.

"My project is going to be totally voltageous!" Frankie declares as she shows Pawla her favorite paint color: lightning-bolt yellow. "I'm doing a glow-in-the-dark portrait of all my Monster High friends."

"I can't wait to see." Pawla is getting more and more excited about the art show. The creativity is catching!

Frankie's paint-covered T-shirt gives Pawla an idea for a poltergeist polka-dot pattern. If only she were old enough to make it right now.

"I'll do a portrait of you! And Clawdeen too!" Frankie promises before she hurries off to work.

In the library, Pawla finds Mr. Dracula working on a collage. He's using old photos from vampire history books. His spectacles are pushed all the way up his nose as he cuts out a picture of a bat.

Pawla is impressed, but she knows better than to disturb him. She tiptoes out of the library quietly. She also likes to have quiet while she works on her jewelry. It helps her focus.

*Maybe all my brothers are in the Creepeteria*, she thinks. *They're always hungry.*

But the Creepeteria is full of Monster

High students preparing for the art show. Deuce and Bonesy are practicing chords for a new song—and taking breaks for snacks.

"Jam on this!" Deuce throws a peanut butter and bogberry jelly sandwich to his friend. Then he continues tuning his guitar.

The sandwich passes right through Bonesy's rib cage! Both mansters laugh and high-five each other.

"Great shot!" Bonesy congratulates Deuce.

*"Great shot!"* sings Deuce, echoing his friend. "What if our song was about monster sports?"

"Oh yeah!" Bonesy agrees, beating his finger bones on a drum.

Pawla grins and does a little dance to the beat of the music. The older mansters clap.

"You could use hockey sticks as drum

sticks and Frisbees as cymbals!" Pawla suggests.

"Clawesome! You're pretty creative," Deuce realizes. "What are *you* doing for the art show?"

"I'm too young to participate," explains Pawla. "But it's still fun to help out."

Across the Creepeteria, Pawla's good ghoulfriend Fangelica is busy baking. She's elbow deep in a mixing bowl. Her face is covered in flour.

Fangelica notices her friend. "Hi, Pawla!" She wipes her forehead. She leaves behind a streak of powdered sugar. "I'm making some cookies. I figure everyone is going to be super hungry when they finish their projects."

"I bet they'll be totally tasty!" Pawla grins and helps her friend put the cookies on a baking sheet. Fangelica may be too young to take classes, just like Pawla, but she's still the best baker at Monster High.

Pawla looks out the window. Abbey Bominable is chiseling an ice sculpture on the lawn. She's wearing protective goggles. *Those are frightfully functional but not fashionable*, Pawla decides. *I would add some ice-white diamonds to the frames and make the strap out of satin.*

She's watching Abbey add the finishing touch to the big round sculpture when she hears familiar voices, coming from the lawn beyond Abbey's work zone.

It's her werebrothers! They are playing a game of Fetch. All of them are completely covered in mud. Barker's clothes are ripped at the knees, and his hair is full of twigs.

"Hey! Pawla!" He notices his sister in the

window. "Come play with us! We miss you! Where have you been?"

"Do you want to help me paint my claws?" Pawla calls over to her brother. "Or make earrings? Or maybe you would let me give you a new hairstyle?"

Barker touches his hair nervously. "Maybe...but I promised our brothers I'd finish this game," Barker explains. "You should join! It will be really fun."

Pawla shakes her head and her brother's ears droop. Barker looks disappointed. A stick flies through the air and Barker runs behind the bushes after it. An instant later, he is at his sister's side, panting.

"Have you heard about Mom's art show?" he asks his sister. "It's such a good idea. Everyone at Monster High has a secret talent."

"I know," Pawla answers, thinking of all the projects she has seen. "I wish we weren't too young to participate. I have some spooky ideas." It is hard not to feel left out sometimes. She sniffs, trying to hide her disappointment.

"Yeah." Barker nods. "Clawdeen's idea is clawesome! She's doing a fashion show." Barker attempts to pat down his wild hair. But he only makes it stand up straighter. He looks like a complete beast!

Pawla nods in agreement as she takes a comb from her dress pocket. Barker blushes with embarrassment as his sister combs down his hair. "I just went to see her in the art room," Pawla says. "Her styles are really coming together. But they're too big for me or you to wear." She looks at her brother, giggling. She can't do anything with his hair. "You're wild, Barker. You look like a wolf!"

"I'm just good at playing Fetch," insists Barker. "You've got to slip and slide in order to catch the stick. There's a real art to it."

Pawla nods, but she's back to thinking about the art show. Barker can tell his sister is distracted. He can tell that she is a little sad.

"What if I go ask Clawdeen if we can help?" he suggests.

"Um..." Pawla bites her lip. She thinks for a second. She knows if Barker comes with her, then *all* her brothers will also come along. And that's a lot of werepups! Her brothers are lots of fun, but they *always* make a mess. What if they ruin Clawdeen's work?

"Thanks, Barker...but I think it's best if

I go fang out with Clawdeen on my own this time," she finally decides.

Barker's face falls. He dusts off his shirt and shrugs. "Okay. I understand, sis."

He watches his sister head off toward the art room. It's hard not to feel a little left out.

*I wish my sisters knew I was old enough to play with them,* Barker thinks. *What I can do to show them I'm not a little pup anymore?*

## CHAPTER 4

# Cut from the Same Cloth

"Not the clay!" gasps Mrs. Wolf.

Gob burps and smiles. He's just eaten a block of molding clay.

"That was the last of it." Mrs. Wolf sighs. She has been trying for hours to help Gob think of what to do for the art show. But he keeps eating up all her ideas!

Gob doesn't seem to mind. Mrs. Wolf is giving him lots of snacks. He pats his big, round belly. So far he's eaten a box of crayons, construction paper, and a new set of paints. If he keeps going, the art room is going to run out of supplies.

"If only we could think of an art project you are *supposed* to eat!" Mrs. Wolf laughs.

"Mom! What's wrong?" asks Clawdeen.

She's stopped by the art room with her ghoulfriends Frankie and Draculaura. They can tell that Mrs. Wolf needs some help.

"Gob keeps gobbling up all my good ideas," Mrs. Wolf explains. "I'm trying to help him figure out a project for the art show."

Gob burps, and paint-covered bubbles come out of his mouth. He smiles. He bursts one of the bubbles with his fingers.

"How frightfully difficult." Draculaura is sympathetic. "But I've got an idea."

"Really?" Mrs. Wolf perks up. "Any ideas are welcome. Especially ones that Gob can't eat."

"Gob, why don't you help me with my video project?" Draculaura asks Gob. "I need someone to help me set up my equipment."

Gob grins. He seems excited by the idea.

"What if we filmed Gob too?" Frankie adds. "We could cover him in some of my glow-in-the-dark paints and film him at night."

"Gob's going to be a star!" Clawdeen claps her hands together. Gob also claps. He is delighted that he's going to be part of the art show. He also wonders what refreshments are going to be served.

"I just hope he doesn't eat your paint, Frankie." Mrs. Wolf chuckles.

"Speaking of my video, do you guys want to see some of the footage I just shot?" Draculaura asks her friends. "Now that I've captured some really good material, I'm ready to share."

The ghouls crowd around their friend. Draculaura takes out her iCoffin. "I want my movie to show how talented everyone is at Monster High. I've been learning a lot about different monster passions in the process." Draculaura shows them a clip of Ari and Operetta singing a new song called "Haunted Harmonies" and another of Lagoona painting with watercolors.

"That's so weird..." Clawdeen says, looking at the clips closely. "Are you ghouls seeing what I'm seeing?"

Everyone peers at the screen. What does Clawdeen see?

Oh, it's obvious.

"Pawla is in every video," Draculaura realizes.

"And she looks really, really sad," Frankie adds.

Sure enough, Pawla is in the background of *all* the monster art project clips. She's frowning and her curls are drooping. She looks lonely.

*Sniff, sniff...sniff.*

"What's that noise?" Frankie asks.

There's sniffling coming from somewhere. All the ghouls look around. Draculaura turns off her iCoffin. The sound isn't coming from her video clips.

"Pawla!" Clawdeen sees her little sister peeking into the art room. She looks even sadder than she did in Draculaura's video footage. She isn't even wearing any accessories! Clawdeen knows that's not a good sign.

"What's wrong, Pawla?" Clawdeen asks her little sister. "You seem like you've been defanged." She thought Pawla was hanging out with Barker. Why is her little sister alone... and unhappy?

"I'm sorry, sis," Pawla apologizes. "I don't mean to mope. The art show just seems so exciting! I've got ideas for fright frames, purses for paws, and day-to-night dresses. I really wish I could help out...."

The older ghouls look at one another. What can they do to cheer up poor Pawla? Monster High is all about making sure everyone is involved. Can they find a way to include Pawla in the art show?

## CHAPTER 5

# In Spooky Style

"I think I've got a creative solution," suggests Mrs. Wolf. She's just finished a fearleading outfit for Clawdeen's fashion show. A shiny bronze spider is embroidered on the top.

All the ghouls look at their art teacher. She picks up a set of pom-poms that go with the outfit. She puts them on her head like a headband. The ghouls all laugh. Mrs. Wolf is such a wacky werewolf!

“Cool accessory, right? But what if Pawla added even better accessories to Clawdeen’s fashion show?” she asks.

“Me? Help with the fashion show? Really?” Pawla is so excited she can’t stay still. She starts to hop up and down. That’s what she wanted all along!

“I bet you have some great ideas. You have an eye for extra-special finishing touches,” Mrs. Wolf continues. One of the pom-poms falls off her head, and she catches it just before it hits the floor.

“Definitely!” Pawla is already planning. “I could make hats with wolf ears attached and rhinestone sunglasses and fake-fur infinity scarves.”

“Oh no. . . .” Clawdeen is frowning. She looks disappointed.

"What?" All the ghouls turn to look at the wereghoul.

"That's an amazing idea. But I've already completely finished my fashion show. I'm sorry," Clawdeen apologizes. "There's nothing left to do."

"That's too bad. I have so many trends I want to try out." Pawla puts her head in her paws. "I guess I'll just have to wait for the art show next year."

Draculaura taps her chin. What can she do to help out Pawla? She nudges her best friend.

"Clawdeen, I've got an idea," she declares. "What if Pawla puts on her *own* fashion show? A fashion show specifically for little-sister styles?"

"But I thought I was too young to

participate," pipes up Pawla. She looks confused.

"That's an idea," Clawdeen says slowly. She nods. "Pawla is handy with a glue gun and cobweb thread. And her dress designs are fangtastic!"

"I *did* make this dress," Pawla notes, pointing to her striped outfit. She has plenty of designs and ideas in her notebooks. She's always reading *Fashionably Fierce* magazine and taking notes.

Mrs. Wolf sighs, thinking. She realizes that she has made a big mistake—and it's time to apologize. She smiles at her daughters. "I was wrong to limit the art show to older students," she admits. "It sounds like the little mansters and ghouls have more than enough talent to do their own projects."

"Really, Mom?" Pawla claps her hands together in excitement.

"Definitely! I think it's a monsterrific idea. We should have included you from the very beginning," Mrs. Wolf continues. "Monster High is about including *everyone.* It's always more fun when everyone is involved."

"I have a feeling Pawla's fashion show is going to be clawesome!" agrees Clawdeen.

"Maybe you older ghouls will even learn something from your younger brothers and sisters," Mrs. Wolf says to Clawdeen and her friends.

Pawla isn't listening. She's already gathering up ribbons and bows. "I can't wait to get started!"

She jumps up and down. She's got to go pick up her dress designs! Maybe she can use her jewelry in the show too. Pawla is sure that her designs are going to be super stylish for little sisters!

## CHAPTER 6

# Seamless

"Hey, Pawla! What are all those notebooks for?" Fangelica asks her ghoulfriend.

Pawla is sitting in the Coffin Café, sipping a Mummy Mocha. She's looking over all her notebooks. There are drawings for a dress made out of cobwebs and skirts woven from branches. She's designed a pearly-white spectral sweater. She's dreamed up some hair clips that look like moths and spiders. She even designed a dress that's half-fake-fur and half-silk. Pawla secretly hopes she can model that one herself. It's supposed to be for a wereghoul changing into a wolf on a full-moon night.

"I'm getting ready for my little-sister fashion show!" exclaims Pawla. She holds out an illustration of a little vampire wearing a jean jacket covered in pink bats.

"Creeptastic!" Fangelica is delighted. "I'd *definitely* wear that!"

"Cool! You can be one of my models," Pawla decides. "But first I've got to *make* these dresses. It's going to be fun. But it will take a lot of work."

"What do you need?" Fangelica asks.

"Um..." Pawla flips through a notebook. "Sparkles and silk and cobwebs and tree branches... and... buttons!"

Fangelica laughs. "Don't worry! I'm sure if we work together we can find all the style supplies we need."

The two ghouls finish their Mummy Mochas and start their supply search.

"Let's check the library," suggests Pawla.

Pawla and Fangelica are careful to step lightly into the dusty room. They don't want to disturb any studious monsters.

But somebody isn't bothering to be quiet. Some monster is whistling a Transylvanian pop tune behind the bookshelves.

"Dad?" Fangelica calls. "Is that you?"

"Mr. Dracula?" questions Pawla.

"*Ahh!* Who?"

The books fall off the shelf and up puffs a cloud of dust. A pair of glasses clatters to the ground at the ghouls' feet. A bat flies around the library several times before landing in front of them and turning into the vampire principal.

"Hi!" the ghouls greet Dracula.

"Sorry! I didn't mean to be so scared. I was totally absorbed in my research," he apologizes. Dracula picks up his glasses and wipes them off before putting them back on. "Cool dress, Pawla!"

"Thanks!" Pawla beams, spinning around. "I made it myself! And I'm going to make *a lot* more."

"Dad, Pawla is putting on a fashion show," Fangelica tells her vampire father. "We're looking for style supplies!"

He wrinkles his brow in thought. "*Hmm.* I might have something interesting for you ghouls."

He disappears behind the bookshelves again but returns a moment later. His arms are full of old parchment and leather-bound manuscripts.

"What are those?" Pawla asks curiously. She takes one off the top of the pile and begins to flip through it. There are pictures of ancient castles and pyramids.

"These papers are history! Monster history to be precise," Dracula tells the little ghouls. "But these are extra copies. And they are full of great illustrations and maps."

"They would look great printed on a dress!" Pawla is thinking out loud. "Imagine a skirt with an old map of Monster High! Thanks, Mr. Dracula!"

"Exactly!" Dracula is beaming. "Glad I could help."

The ghouls eagerly take the papers and manuscripts. They wave good-bye to their Monster High teacher.

"Trust Dad to turn everything into a history lesson, even a stylish dress!" jokes Fangelica as they leave the library.

It turns out everyone has something to give to the ghouls. Ms. Kindergrubber gives them leftover lace from when she made tablecloths in her Home Ick class. Frankie donates a couple of cans of glow-in-the-dark paint.

Fangelica notices Lagoona Blue on a stepladder near the entrance to the Creepeteria. She is finishing her watercolor display for the art show. It's a scene of monsters and ghouls having an underwater tea party.

"How beautiful!" Pawla exclaims.

"Hey, guys!" Lagoona greets them. "I heard about your fashion show. Need some materials?"

"Definitely!" the ghouls both agree.

Lagoona comes down from her stepladder and dries off her hands on a towel. Crazy colors streak her arms.

"Could you use some of these?" Lagoona says as she gives Pawla a bag full of coral beads and seashells. "I was going to paste them onto my painting. But now that I'm almost finished, I don't think I need them."

"I'll make a necklace with these beads," says Pawla. She glances at Lagoona's apron. It's speckled with watercolors. It gives her an idea! "I might even do a to-die-for tie-dye T-shirt based on your apron. "

Lagoona looks down in surprise. Then she grins. "You're so creative, Pawla. That's an absolutely oceanic idea."

"I can't wait to see all these finished fashions," Fangelica responds with excitement. She can't believe Pawla is going to let her actually model these special outfits.

The ghouls head back to the art room with their supplies. The room is full of fabrics, feathers, and fake fur.

"It's time to begin!" Pawla says with delight as she takes out her designs. "I think we have everything we need to make a super-stylish little-sister show."

"You need ice? I bring ice!" Abbey declares as she pops through the door.

"Thanks!" Pawla says, holding out her hands. But the icicles are almost melted. They slip and slide through her fingers. A puddle forms on the floor.

"Oops...." Abbey tries to clean up the mess. But her long silvery-blue hair gets wet.

"Don't worry about it!" Fangelica laughs.

"Why don't we make *fake* icicles out of frosting? I have a great frosting recipe. I think it could look really realistic."

Abbey nods when she realizes the ice won't last until the art show. "But I know best stuffing for warm snowsuits. Puffier better. You make waterproof too. Must soak suit in yak butter." Abbey lists several more tips and tells the ghouls to check back in if they have any questions.

"This is so much fun!" declares Fangelica. She starts to pin some strips of silk to a little monster mannequin. "I love working alongside friends. It's just as good as being old enough to take a Monster High class. I'm learning so much about sewing and style from you!"

Pawla smiles at her friend. She's finishing an outfit with an antennae visor and big metallic wings.

"Those wings are flytastic!" Fangelica declares. "I wish mine were as colorful as those."

Pawla is having a great time. And almost everybody at Monster High has contributed something to her fashion show. Everyone, that is, except the werepups.

Pawla has been so busy searching for supplies and planning for the fashion show with Fangelica that she's completely forgotten about her little brothers.

## CHAPTER 7

# Heart on a Sleeve

"You tighten the loop. And then you take the thread and do the same step again," explains Pawla. She's teaching Fangelica how to crochet lace out of some cobwebs Webby just dropped off.

Pawla holds out her own finished piece of lace. It's picture-perfect.

"Oops!" Fangelica tries to follow the steps but ends up tangling her threads.

Pawla laughs and takes the crochet needle from her friend.

"Don't worry! You'll get the hang of it soon. Practice makes perfect." Pawla easily fixes the small mistake.

"Wouldn't it be trendy to do a sleep-style section of the show?" suggests Fangelica. "We could add this lace to the bottom of a Coffin Dreams nightgown."

"Nightgown?" Pawla laughs. "You mean *day*gown!"

Fangelica laughs and starts to sew up a Transylvanian tutu. The skirt is woven with brambles and bogberries.

"Where did you learn so much about sewing and style?" Fangelica asks Pawla. They are pinning their finished lace onto the monster mannequin. The outfits are beginning to come together. "You could easily teach your own Monster High class on fashion."

"Maybe I'll be a teacher one day. Just like my mom!" Pawla says. "My older sister, Clawdeen, knows all sorts of stitches and sewing tricks. She taught me the basics. But Dracula also found me some books on dressmaking. They were super helpful."

Her voice trails off. She's distracted by a loud roaring noise. Someone is pounding down the door!

*Bang! Bang! Bang!*

Who could it be?

Fangelica leaps up and opens the door just before it breaks. Barker and all the werepups stream into the room. They jump over one another. They bump into the mannequins and knock them down. They take turns chasing one another around the room. They've finally found their sister!

"Werewhoops!" cries Pawla as she pulls away some lace from one of her brothers. He's unraveling all her careful work! She's about to snap at him when she remembers something. Something important. Oops!

"I'm so sorry!" Pawla apologizes. "I forgot I was going to fang out with you pups. I've been so busy with my fashion show."

"Hey, sis!" Barker bounds up to his sister. He gives Pawla such a big hug that she almost falls over.

"I brought some twigs and leaves for a swamp monster hat. Could you use these? Can we help out?" asks Barker. Overexcited, he picks up a half-finished genie jacket.

It's covered in long silvery threads and glittering jewels. "This looks super cool. Can I try it on?"

Before Pawla has time to answer, Barker has his arms in the jacket. But it's too small for Barker, and the jacket starts to rip at the seams!

"No! Don't put it on!" exclaims Pawla. She takes a deep breath, trying to calm down. "I mean, it's not for you. That is a jacket for a *much* smaller little-sister ghoul," she explains.

She takes the jacket back from Barker and shoots him a stern look. "These styles are for ghouls, not mansters."

Barker looks bashful. "Sorry, sis. I'll try to be more careful."

But Fangelica is having a great time with the werepups. "Your brothers are so much fun," Fangelica tells Pawla, laughing. She's spinning ribbons around one of the mannequins with the help of two werepups. Another brother is chewing up all the fake fur. Scales and glitz and sparkly scarves are flying everywhere! The art room doesn't look like a fashion workshop! It looks like a werewolf playroom.

Pawla is very upset. She's overwhelmed. "Do you want to help, Barker?" she asks her brother. "You can help by calming down these puppies!"

Barker looks around helplessly. There are werepups everywhere. Where should he begin?

"Why don't you give them a specific job?" suggests Fangelica. "Then they'll be too busy to make a mess."

Pawla nods. That could work. She asks her brothers to organize the box full of ancient Egyptian buttons.

"We're on it!" Barker is glad to have something to do. He herds the brothers into a circle. He has them settle down and sit around the button box.

For a minute it seems as if Fangelica's suggestion is a success! Almost all the buttons are organized in little bags.

*Maybe my brothers aren't so beastly after all...* thinks Pawla.

But in no time the werepups have lost interest in their task. They don't have a long attention span. They start to play Fetch with a pincushion. As they run and jump around, they end up spilling the button bags they just organized.

*"Ahh!"* Pawla cries, dodging the prickly projectile. "Watch out where you throw that thing!"

"Sorry!" Barker apologizes. He grabs the pincushion away from his younger brother and pats him on the head. "Let's find something else to do, buddy."

Next, Fangelica gives the werepups some dress patterns to cut out.

Pawla is still hopeful that her brothers can start making something instead of breaking everything. It's fun to be able to share some of her passions with them for once. She's usually tagging along as they play games instead. Isn't it time for them to do what she wants for a change? She smiles as she watches them happily cutting out paper patterns for a static-resistant zombie hoodie.

But the second she leaves them alone and starts sewing up a waterproof skirt, the brothers are back to their mischief. They're playing tug-of-tail with a long piece of silk.

"It's mine!"

"No, mine!" the werepups argue.

"Watch out!" Pawla tries to save the piece of silk. But she's too late. It rips right down the middle, and the brothers all fall down in a puppy pile.

"What a mess!" Pawla throws up her hands in distress. Her brothers are way too crazy to help out.

Fangelica sees that her friend is upset.

"They are just silly," Fangelica says, excusing them. She wishes she had lots of brothers. Pawla's brothers make her laugh. One of the werepups is scratching his ear while another chases his tail. "They can be our entertainment while we finish our fashions," she suggests.

"They turn everything into a game!" complains Pawla. "And this isn't a game. It's a *real* fashion show."

"That's true," Fangelica agrees with her friend. She nods sympathetically. "We all want Mrs. Wolf's art show to be a super success."

"That means we have to take our work seriously," Pawla says, stomping her foot. "I usually love fanging out with my brothers. But this isn't fanging out! This isn't playtime!"

*Bang!*

One of the youngest werepups knocks over a box of safety pins. Another werepup is hanging from the ceiling light on a long string of pearls that's about to snap.

What is Pawla going to do with her brothers? She needs to get her work done! Most of all, she needs Clawdeen and her mother to finally understand that she's mature enough to participate in Monster High activities.

## CHAPTER 8

# A Perfect Fit?

*Calm your claws*, Pawla tells herself as she tidies up the art room. Fangelica has convinced her to give her brothers one more chance. The two ghouls decided to let the little pups glue scales to a waterproof ballroom gown. The gown is going to be shimmery blue. Pawla wants the skirt to move across the runway like river water. She knows it's going to look gore-geous on

Kelpie. She just hopes her brothers do not ruin it.

"Look! Your brothers are being useful," Fangelica points out. She's finishing lacing up a pair of high-heeled snow boots. "With more helping hands, we can finish this fashion show way ahead of schedule. Clawdeen will be really impressed."

Pawla grins. Maybe having her brothers around isn't so bad after all. They've already fixed the final row of scales onto the skirt. Kelpie's outfit is almost finished!

"Help me button up this frosted blazer?" asks Fangelica. She's attached frosting icicles to the collar. The blazer looks fangtastically frozen!

There's a scuffle going on behind the ghouls. They pause their work and look around.

"Give it back!"

"No! Give it to me!"

"No fair!"

"Oh no." Pawla sighs. It sounds like her brothers are back to being beasts.

Sure enough, she spots the werepups rip the gown in two! The sequins scatter everywhere.

"Glamorous ghosts, gremlins, and ghouls!" exclaims Fangelica.

It seems as if the brothers are in a fight about who would add the last scale. But they've ended up tearing all their good work apart. The gown is totally in shreds.

"What are we going to do?" Pawla despairs.

Barker is trying to calm down his brothers.

"Please keep your paws to yourself! Can't you see our sister needs help?"

"Help? Help! I want to play a game!" says a werepup. He's bouncing up and down with energy.

"That's it!" Pawla puts her foot down. It's time to take control of this chaos. She needs to finish her fashion show. "You guys are way too wild to help out. Can you give me space?" she asks her brothers.

Barker is disappointed. He wants to help out. He has lots of good ideas to make the fashion show a hit—baseball beast caps, creature-covered kerchiefs, flying book bags. But he's been too busy trying to control the werepups to share them with Pawla. Does she think he's part of the problem?

"It doesn't make sense for you guys to help anyway," Pawla is saying. "This fashion show is for *girly* ghouls, not *beastly* mansters."

"I've always wanted to be a beast.

*Awoo!*" One of the brothers howls like a wolf. "Can we play a beast game?"

"No!" Pawla shakes her head. "This room is for designing only. You guys can play games anywhere else in Monster High."

Barker sees that his sister is upset. He calms down his brothers and leads them out of the art room. Maybe he can keep them busy with a werewolf wrestling match.

"Pawla?" He turns to his sister before he closes the door. "I'm sorry. I really *did* want to help out with your show."

Pawla knows Barker is telling the truth. But she's still frustrated. She's lost so much time. She needs to focus if she's going to finish all her styles in time for the art show.

"I know," she tells him. "But I need to get to work, Barker. I promise we'll fang out later." She turns on her sewing machine.

Barker nods. He loves his sister. He wishes he didn't have to leave. The art show would be so much more fun if they could work together! If only he could convince her to let him stay and fang out.

## CHAPTER 9

# Monster Mod

"It's a shame that I didn't get to share any of my creeperific ideas with my sister," Barker says as he wanders through the howlway. "Her fashions are cool but not clawesome. Together we could make styles that are totally unique. She needs some mud and gooey globs . . . things that some mansters like too!"

But no one is listening to him.

"Barker! Come join in our game of hide-and-creep!" one of his little brothers calls from the castle's front door.

Barker gives his brother a smile, but he waves him away. "I'll join later! You guys can start the game without me."

Barker has played *a lot* of hide-and-creep lately. He loves his brothers, but he misses fanging out with Pawla. He wishes she weren't so busy! This fashion show has really gotten in the way of their friendship.

Painting claws and hairstyling doesn't sound so bad now. Barker wants to try something new.

*If Pawla doesn't have time to fang out, maybe my sister Clawdeen is free,* Barker thinks. *I can tell* her *about the cool clothes I want to make.*

Where is his sister? Clawdeen isn't in the

Coffin Café. She's not in the Creepeteria, either! But she is outside with Abbey Bominable setting up her ice sculpture booth.

"Let's add some sparkly streamers up here," Clawdeen is saying to Abbey. She's pinning some silvery streamers to the top of Abbey's booth. There are ice packs set up all around the sculptures to keep them frozen.

"Hey, big sis!" says Barker.

"Hi, Barker! What's up?" Clawdeen is happy to see her brother.

"Oh, nothing. I was just wondering if you could help me glue some scales to my sock—"

"No time! Must finish booth before ice melts!" Abbey interrupts. "Need Clawdeen's help!"

Clawdeen laughs. "Don't worry, Abbey.

I won't leave until your booth is totally frozen. I've got a bunch more ice packs in the fridge that we can use to keep these icicles icy."

"Good, good." Abbey breathes a frosty sigh of relief.

"Sorry, Barker," Clawdeen apologizes. "I've got to help set up the art show. But I would love to work on some styles with you. Maybe tomorrow?"

Barker nods. "That's okay! I guess I'll go look for Mom."

"Try the Home Ick room," Clawdeen suggests. "I saw her there last."

Sure enough, Mrs. Wolf is in the Home Ick room. But she's totally tied up.

"Sorry, Barker," Mrs. Wolf says as she tries to untangle herself from a ball of yarn as big as a pumpkin. "I have to help these students straighten out their knitting projects. But let's cook dinner together later? Fang-fried rice and veggies?"

"Okay. Good luck!" Barker hopes his mom's art show is a success. He watches her trying to untangle one of Deuce Gorgon's hair snakes from the yarn. He shakes his head. Mrs. Wolf has a lot to do. He sighs. His whole family is so busy with the art show.

Barker is beginning to feel left out. Maybe he should just play with his brothers after all.

The werepups are finishing their game of hide-and-creep on the front lawn. They have grass and leaves stuck in their hair. Their feet are covered in mud.

"Barker! You missed the best game!" the littlest pup calls to him.

"Yeah! The best!" says another brother.

"Can I play in the next one?" he asks.

"Definitely!" his brothers answer together. One of them picks up a sock from the ground and puts it on top of his head. It looks like a really silly hat. All the brothers laugh.

"Hey!" Barker exclaims. "That gives me a beastly idea."

"This sock? Really?" his brother asks. "It doesn't even have a pair!"

"It doesn't matter." Barker grins. "It's a hat!"

All the brothers look at Barker in confusion. What is he talking about?

"A manster show! With manster hats and suits and jackets!" Barker explains. He picks up a discarded scarf from the ground and ties it around his waist.

"That's a cool belt!" says one of the werepups.

"I'd definitely wear that," adds another.

"But what if the belt looked like a snake? And what if we made neckties that growl and bark and howl like wolves?" Barker claps in excitement. He gathers up his brothers and leads them back into the castle. They don't have any time to spare. If they want to be ready for the art show, they have to start working immediately.

"If I can't be a part of my sister's ghoul fashion show, then I'll have my own," Barker declares. "A little-*manster* fashion show!"

## CHAPTER 10

# If the Shoe Fits

"This is almost as fun as baking!" Fangelica is sewing a ghost gown. She is almost done. Pawla is a great teacher. Her stitches are getting smaller and straighter.

Pawla nods in agreement. She's gluing some glitter to a crown covered in hieroglyphs. It's going to be part of Pharrah de Nile's fashion show outfit. She's a little nervous about outfitting her stylish ghoulfriend. She knows Pharrah won't wear any old mummy wrapping.

"Yeah. This is so much fun!" Pawla says, grinning. "And it's so cool that we get to involve all the other little sisters."

Pawla and Fangelica have talked to all the little sisters. They are making special outfits for each of them to model! Kelpie will wear a sparkly scuba suit for her first walk down the runway. Then she will model a boo-tiful blue gown that Pawla wants to look like flowing water. Alivia's dress is going to be covered in lights that blink and flash different colors. Pawla is secretly working on a cupcake-patterned tutu for Fangelica. It's going to have an apron attached so Fangelica can wear it while she bakes.

"I can't believe we're almost done!" exclaims Pawla as she stands back to admire their work. The art room is filled with finished dresses, skirts, and hats.

"Definitely. We work really well together." Fangelica slips the finished ghost gown onto a monster mannequin.

Both ghouls take a moment to examine their creations. There is an outfit for every little sister.

Pawla frowns. She taps her chin with a painted claw.

"What is it?" asks Fangelica. "Did I miss a button? Is there an unzipped zipper?"

"No. Everything's perfect," Pawla responds, still frowning. "Everything's perfectly fine."

Fine. But not amazing. That's what she is thinking. "Something is missing," she says out loud.

Fangelica takes another look at the styles

on the monster mannequins. All the fashions are done. *Is Pawla right?* Functional but not fangtastic. Ghoulish but not glamorous. Spooky but not spooktacular. It's true. They are missing...something. But what?

Pawla picks up a pair of platform booties. They are made from platypus pleather. She turns them around in her hands. "How can we make our show more special?" she asks.

Fangelica thinks hard. She doesn't know. "Maybe we just have to add a cobweb here and a cobweb there," she suggests. She drapes some cobwebs over a black velvet cape, but it looks dingy, not dazzling.

Meanwhile Pawla is painting a lightning bolt onto the high-heeled boots. It looks totally okay, but that's it.

"I can't shake the feeling that I'm not

seeing something," Pawla complains. She shakes her head. "Nothing is original or exciting enough."

"Don't be so hard on yourself," Fangelica reassures her ghoulfriend. "It's really cool that we put together a little-sister fashion show."

"I know." Pawla is still frowning. "But I've got the same feeling I get when a necklace isn't done. I always know when my jewelry needs an extra bead or jewel."

Fangelica can't argue with Pawla's artistic eye. She's definitely right. The fashion show is in need of some extra-special finishing touches. She knows when a recipe needs a little of this and a little of that, but when it comes to fashion, her closet is empty.

Someone is knocking at the art room door. It's Kelpie!

"Hi, guys!" says Lagoona Blue's little sister. Her glasses are crooked. She pushes them back on her nose and comes into the room. "I don't mean to interrupt, but I have huge news."

"What?" Pawla and Fangelica ask together.

"I was just in the Creepeteria, and I ran into Barker and the rest of your brothers."

"Were they playing a game?" Pawla asks in frustration.

"No!" Kelpie's eyes go wide. "They were bragging about their super-cool styles."

"Styles?" Pawla and Fangelica are both confused.

"Yeah!" Kelpie continues. "Styles for their art show project. Barker is putting on his very own little-manster fashion show!"

Pawla can't believe her ears. That's just

what she needs—a competition. How will she ever stand out? She shakes her head in frustration. She needs to talk to her brothers. Immediately. Barker is acting like a complete wolf!

CHAPTER 11

# What Not to Wear

"Not only are the boots waterproof but they have claws," Pawla overhears her brother saying. "We're going to make them in a bunch of sizes." His voice is coming from inside the Monster High library.

Pawla peeks inside the library. Barker is boasting about his fashion show to a bunch of monsters. Toralei is paying close attention and Bonesy is nodding in encouragement. Everyone is asking questions. Is he going to have manster models? Is his show *part* of Pawla's show?

"Clawed boots?" asks Pawla, walking into the library. "I didn't know you wore shoes, Barker. Aren't you always barefoot?"

Barker blushes. He *is* barefoot. It makes it easier for him to run outside during games of Fetch.

"That doesn't matter!" he responds. "These boots are for other mansters. We'll have deep-sea flippers and roller skates for wraiths too!"

Pawla feels bad about embarrassing her brother. After all, he *is* her best friend. But why is he competing with her? Why is he doing a fashion show too?

"Are you guys working together?" Alivia asks Barker. "I thought Pawla was in charge of the little-sibling styles."

"No!" both Barker and Pawla answer at once. They turn to look at each other, surprised.

"I mean—I mean—" Pawla stammers.

"Pawla doesn't need any help with her girly-ghoul show," Barker interrupts. "So I'm doing my own fashion show. It's only manster styles."

"Cool, dude!" Rayth exclaims. He's been looking up chords in a book of sheet music. He closes the book and nods encouragingly. "It would be even cooler if you made some styles for bigger mansters too."

"Definitely!" Barker agrees. "Our deep-sea-diving wet-suit tuxedos are going to come in a couple of different sizes. And I've got a plan for a line of skele-neckties that any manster can wear."

Deep-sea diving tuxedos? Clawed boots? Barker's fashion ideas are so creative. Pawla is worried her brother's show is going to outshine her little-sister styles.

"My designs come in all sizes. But I don't want to spoil the surprise. You guys will see them all at the art show!" Pawla declares.

Barker crosses his arms. "Game on!"

"Okay!" Pawla huffs. "I guess we'll just have to wait and see whose show is the most fashionably fierce."

She turns and heads out the door, back to the art room. But she isn't happy. It's one thing to compete against each other in a game of Fetch... and another when the whole school is watching to see who will succeed and who might fail.

Back in the art room, she studies her designs and shakes her head. Her fashions just don't have flair. The dresses look as dull as something a Normie might wear.

*Thunk!*

A big red jewel falls off Pharrah de Nile's crown and rolls across the floor. Pawla sighs.

If only she and Barker were working together. His creativity and her designs are a perfect fit. They would make a great team.

## CHAPTER 12

# Spinning a Yarn

Barker trudges upstairs to the attic. He is feeling upset. He does not want to have a competition with his sister. He wants them to work together. He wants to help her. What should he do?

A howl, a crash, and a loud *BOOM!* interrupt his thoughts.

A cloud of cotton balls and pom-poms flies through the doorway. Barker sneezes.

"What is going on?" he cries as he looks around his studio.

Barker left the werepups with strict orders to organize all their manster materials. He gave them boxes of bog weeds to weave together and mummy wrapping to untangle. But the brothers have not been organizing anything. They've been *dis*organizing!

"Here!" A pup throws a ball of yarn across the room. It smashes into an old mirror.

"Stop! Stop! Stop!" Barker cries. "This isn't a game! This is a fashion show!"

"What?" all the brothers ask in unison, confused.

"Really?" one of them calls out. The pups look disappointed, but they begin to calm down. One hops down off an old bookcase. The bookcase wobbles before falling over on top of Barker's cobweb-thread sewing machine. *Cr...ack.*

"Oh no." Barker puts his head in his hands. "I guess I'll have to stitch by paw from here on out."

Barker had talked a big game in the library. Sure, he has great ideas. But the truth is that he has no idea at all how to make anything he has imagined. Besides, his brothers are out of control. What is he going to do? "This isn't a game," Barker repeats, upset.

"I thought the fashion show *was* a game," his littlest brother says. He is chewing on a piece of fake fur. "A really, really fun game."

"A really silly game," adds a pup.

"These buttons are delicious!" says another, popping the last of the pearl buttons into his mouth.

"You guys have ruined all the supplies." Barker shakes his head. The mummy wrapping is beyond repair! Maybe he can use it to mop up the glow-in-the-dark paint that's spilled all over the floor? "Will you try to clean up the studio while I look for some more materials?"

They all smile and nod. "Sure, Barker!"

Barker loves his brothers. They mean well, but they can be so immature.

They wave good-bye as he heads down the stairs. He needs to find some spiderwebs and rhinestones and eyeball buttons fast.

Barker tries the Monster High supply room first. But all the big boxes of art supplies and fabric are gone.

*Huh*... he thinks. *I guess Pawla and Clawdeen used everything for their show.*

The Home Ick room is also empty. All the

cobwebs have been unthreaded from the sewing machines. The yarn basket has only one ball left and it's an icky pink color. *Pink is for girly-ghouls*, he grumbles to himself. Barker wants brown or green yarn for his manster designs.

"Claws and coffins!" he exclaims. "How am I going to make my styles without any materials?"

"What's wrong, Barker?" asks Mrs. Wolf. She and Mr. Dracula are carrying tables outside to set up for the art show.

Barker greets them with relief. "Hi! I can't find anything to use to make my skeleton suspenders and bat-wing backpacks. Is there any more fabric left? Do you have glitter glue or clanking chains?"

Mrs. Wolf shakes her head. "I'm sorry, Barker. The fabric and fake fur we gave you were the very last supplies we had! Have you used them all up already?"

Barker is too embarrassed to tell them that his little brothers have eaten up all his style supplies.

"It's okay! I'll think of something." Barker smiles. "Good luck with the art show! I can't wait to see everyone's projects."

The monster adults head off with their heavy tables.

As soon as they are gone, Barker lets the grin drop from his face. He's too worried to smile! What is he going to do? He's told everyone, including Pawla, that his fashion show is going to be extra fancy. But he doesn't even have enough thread to sew up *one* clawed boot.

But that's not the biggest problem. Barker has a few wacky ideas for creepy cuff links and gargoyle-horn headgear, but he doesn't really know how to put together a whole outfit. That's what Pawla is good at.

The werepups have tried to clean up the studio, but it is still very messy. Barker sits down at his crushed sewing machine and sighs. He runs a hand through his messy hair. He doesn't even have his *own* signature style. He picks up a shard of a broken mirror and looks at his reflection.

Beastly! He's got glitter glue on his cheek and fake fur stuck in his hair.

Maybe he's just like his little brothers. Messy. Maybe what he's really good at is getting dirty and playing games.

"Fashion is Pawla's hobby, not mine," he admits to his brothers. "I wish I hadn't bragged about my show to her earlier. Maybe I could have just asked her for help."

"Help? You need help?" one of his brothers asks, jumping up and down. "Let's ask Pawla for help!"

"It's too late." Barker shakes his head. "I'll just have to figure something out. Maybe I'll make a show that doesn't need any materials. The styles will be strictly for ghosts... absolutely invisible!"

## CHAPTER 13

# By Design

"Preparing for the art show has been fun but super time-consuming." Clawdeen sighs as she sits down at the Coffin Café. She finally has a free moment.

She sips her coffinccino. At last, she can catch her breath. Her outfits are all ready to be modeled. Everything has been sewed, glued, fitted, and safety-pinned. Preparing for the art show has been a lot of work.

Clawdeen wonders how her little sister's fashion show is progressing.

*She's so creative*, thinks Clawdeen. *I loved that striped dress she was wearing. Maybe she can make me one just like it. I bet her styles are totally boo-tiful.*

But a little later when Clawdeen knocks on the art room door, Pawla won't let her big sister inside the room.

"I'm sorry, Clawdeen," she says. "My designs aren't good enough for the art show." She hangs her head, embarrassed. She wanted her big sister to be proud of her. But now she is just a disappointment.

Clawdeen doesn't believe her. "I know that's not true. I've seen your dress designs. Look at the one you're wearing! Everything you create is totally unique. All of Monster

High is excited to see your styles stride down the runway," she says encouragingly.

Pawla smiles half-heartedly. "It means a lot that you believe in me. But I *know* something is missing from my styles. I just can't put my claw on what it is."

"Have you asked for help from anyone?" Clawdeen asks.

"Fangelica is helping with everything," answers Pawla. "But she can't figure it out, either. If I were making muffins, she would know what spice to add, but she doesn't have any idea if pleats are missing or I need more frills. That's the kind of thing Barker is good at. But he's busy with his manster show. I bet it's going to be amazing."

Clawdeen taps her high-heeled purple boots. She pulls on one of her hoop earrings.

What can she do to help out her little sister?

"Just because Barker has his own show doesn't mean you can't ask him for his help," she tells Pawla. "It's always important to learn from other monsters, even your own family."

She looks closely at her little sister and thinks about how much she has learned from Pawla. Pawla showed her how to bead delicate firefly-wing necklaces. She even showed her how to twist pieces of spiderweb into chain mail.

"Especially your own family," she adds.

"But Barker seems so competitive!" Pawla cries. "And besides, I want to be independent like you!"

"Like me? Really?" Clawdeen laughs a little. "I needed *so* much help with my show. Mom brought me my supplies, and all my ghoulfriends helped me sew and stitch up my designs. *You* inspired all the jeweled accessories. It's thanks to everyone at Monster High that I finished my project."

Pawla is surprised. She thought Clawdeen created her fashion show completely by herself.

"That makes me feel better," she tells her sister. "I guess maybe I should ask Barker for his opinion. I usually ask him for help with my other projects."

"I think that's a great idea." Clawdeen is happy that her sister and brother are going to work together.

It's true. Barker is Pawla's best friend. She misses his creativity and sense of humor. In fact, she misses *all* her brothers.

## CHAPTER 14

# A Stitch in Time

Barker's iCoffin is sounding an alert. *"Awoo! Awoo! Boo!"* He set up a Creep Camera on the stairs that tells him when someone is coming. He doesn't want anyone sneaking up and stealing his styles . . . even if he doesn't have any styles to steal.

*"Agh!"* Barker exclaims, looking at his iCoffin. "It's my sister!"

He can see Pawla slowly making her way

up the creaky stairs. Oh no! She is going to find out that he hasn't accomplished anything.

"Guys! We have to make this look like a real fashion studio!" Barker instructs his little brothers. "We don't want Pawla to see how far behind we are."

"Why?" asks one of the werepups. He is chewing on the end of a ribbon. "What if we just ask Pawla for help?"

"No!" Barker says fiercely. "She didn't want help with *her* show, and I don't want help, either. I don't need it. I can do this all by myself."

Barker tries to sweep up the mess—the frayed ribbons, the bits and pieces of poltergeist polyester, the chewed-on buttons. The werepups keep sliding into his piles. They think it's a big game. Barker tries to settle them down, and they start chasing one another's tails.

"Barker?" A voice comes from behind the closed door.

*Oh no! Too little too late!* Barker bites his claws. He opens the door a crack and slips out.

"You can't come in," he tells Pawla. "My studio is top secret."

"Really?" Pawla tries to peek over his shoulder. "I'd love to see some of what you are working on. I was wondering if—"

"You can't!" Barker interrupts. "But trust me, these getups are ghastly—I mean, ghostly—I mean, great." He slams the door shut.

Pawla is disappointed. She didn't even have time to ask for Barker's help!

A huge crash startles Pawla! A ball of wrestling werepups bursts through the attic door!

Now that the door is open, Pawla can see into the studio. She blinks in surprise. Then she rubs her eyes.

There aren't any clawed boots or scuba suits. There aren't any chain-mail pants or wraith raincoats or chef uniform getups for Gob.

The only thing Pawla sees is a total mess.

## CHAPTER 15

# Off the Cuff

"This studio is off-limits!" Barker tries to block the doorway with his arms. But Pawla easily slips by her little brother.

There are cobwebs hanging from the ceiling and pincushions lodged in the chandelier. Bits of fluff cover the floor. Scraps of tattered silk and satin pour out of spare coffins. It even looks like a werepup got his paws into some glow-in-the-dark paint and tried finger-painting the walls. There are fashion supplies scattered everywhere. But there isn't a single outfit in sight.

"Where are the clawed boots? The scarecrow hats? The fancy fanged bandannas?" Pawla asks as she peeks under a pile of ribbons covered in tooth marks.

Barker blushes. He hides his face in his paws.

One of the werepups holds up a single sock. There is a hole in the heel.

That's it? Pawla raises an eyebrow and her little brother drops the sock.

"I guess your boasting was all show," Pawla realizes, "because as far as I can see you don't have anything for your models to actually wear in a fashion show!"

Barker hangs his head, upset. His sister has found him out. But that doesn't make Pawla happy at all.

"It's okay, Barker!" She pats his back. "I have a confession."

"Yeah?" Barker blinks up at his sister. "It can't be as embarrassing as my unfinished fashions."

"Well..." Pawla laughs. "My fashions may be finished, but they're definitely not special enough for the art show. I can't figure out what's missing. I was actually coming up to the attic to ask you for your help."

"Really? You were?" Barker starts to cheer up. "You want my help?"

"Yeah! I do." Pawla nods. "I feel like you could add that extra sparkle that will help my styles to shine."

Before Pawla can finish speaking, Barker gives his sister a big, beastly hug. They both topple over. The werepups pile on top of them. They are whooping and cheering happily.

Pawla laughs and dusts off her dress.

"You're all full of energy! Are you okay, Barker?"

"I'm more than okay. I'm clawesome! I'm monsterrific!" cries Barker. "I'd love to help you with your fashion show. That's *actually* what I wanted all along. I never wanted to have my own competing show. I just wanted to fang out with you."

"Really?"

"Really," Barker tells Pawla.

"Me too!" Pawla admits. She's missed her little brother/best friend. "I'm glad we're not competing anymore. It felt weird not talking to you."

All their brothers applaud in agreement.

"But first!" Pawla says, pointing a perfectly polished claw in the air. "We have to clean up this monstrous mess!"

CHAPTER 16

# Noticing a Pattern

"This attic is so messy it's almost a work of art!" Fangelica declares as she looks around Barker's studio. She's winding up yarn into a ball.

Pawla has called her ghoulfriend to help with the cleanup.

"Thanks for coming to the rescue," Barker tells Fangelica. "We need all the help we can get."

"Hey! What's this?" Fangelica asks as she picks up a piece of zebra-printed velvet. Underneath it is a stack of drawings. She picks one up and looks at it closely. It's Kelpie's water gown, but something is different.... She looks at another. She grins, delighted.

They are pictures of dresses Pawla has designed—but Barker has added all kinds of accessories to them. Kelpie's underwater skirt has foam bubbles all along the hemline. A puffy white ghost blouse has a frilled bottom. An electric T-shirt has cutouts of lightning bolts on the sleeves. Even the dress Pawla designed for Fangelica looks better paired with jack-o'-lantern earrings and a kerchief covered in pictures of cupcakes.

"These are amazing," she whispers to herself. And they have given her an idea.

Fangelica waits until the attic is all cleaned up. The little monsters sit back and share some of Fangelica's famous chocolate crypt cookies to celebrate their success.

"Great teamwork!" Pawla high-fives her brothers.

"That reminds me," Fangelica pipes up. "I have a stylish suggestion."

Everyone looks at the vampire ghoul. She blushes. "I noticed how cool Barker's additions were to Pawla's new designs. And it got me thinking. What if you two joined forces and made a fashion show for ghouls *and* mansters?"

Pawla's mouth drops open. Barker's eyes go as big as full moons.

Fangelica bites her lip anxiously.

"Freaky fabulous!" The weresiblings are beaming.

“We’ll make the trendiest team!” declares Pawla.

Barker is jumping up and down in excitement. “It’s what I wanted all along . . . just to help out my sister.”

The siblings are delighted to have their favorite friendship back.

“Let’s get to the studio and start work!” suggests Fangelica. “We don’t have a lot of time before the art show.”

The ghouls head off to the art room.

“Now I know what was missing from my fashion show,” realizes Pawla. “It wasn’t sparkles or buttons or hats. It was my brother all along!”

## CHAPTER 17

# Pleats and Treats

"Wow! These are creeptastic!" a werepup exclaims as he takes a bite of a full-moon cupcake. "They are even better than the ones Mom bakes."

Fangelica smiles. "That's good to hear. Your sister Pawla taught me the recipe. But I've been experimenting with vanilla bean in the frosting."

Fangelica has found a way to distract

the werepups: food! She baked up a batch of full-moon cupcakes and brought them to the art room. As soon as she put them on the table, the werepups pounced on the pastries!

"Yum!" Two werebrothers take a bite from the same cupcake. They shake and tug until it pulls apart! Crumbs scatter everywhere! But at least the brothers are making a mess only in the corner. Pawla and Barker have the rest of the room free for their fashion collaboration.

"Thanks for keeping them quiet," Pawla whispers to her ghoulfriend.

"No problem. But I better keep baking! I need to have more of these ready for the art show—and more for your brothers to eat too," Fangelica says as she looks at the almost-empty cupcake platter.

Fangelica heads off to the kitchen to cook up some more distracting desserts.

"Hey!" Barker calls after his friend, "bring me back one too? All this sewing and stitching is making me hungry!"

Fangelica smiles. "Definitely! You just get to work on my fashion show outfit. I bet it's going to be fangtastic."

Fangelica is right. Pawla and Barker make a great team. Barker has added butterfly-wing bowties, hieroglyph-printed briefcases, and unicorn-horn top hats. His accessories are making Pawla's designs pop. Pawla has been busy sewing up manster outfits. She's especially happy with a hoodie for Deuce Gorgon that has holes for his hair snakes to hiss through.

"What do you think of these skull and

crossbones cargo pants?" she asks her brother, holding up a pair of green pants.

*"Hmm."* Barker studies Pawla's creation. "They look great. But if a skeleton is going to wear them, don't you think they'll need some suspenders?"

"You're right!" Pawla nods. "A skeleton is too skinny to keep up his pants. I didn't even think of that."

Barker is already busy sewing together some skull-patterned suspenders. When he's done, he looks closely at them and then adds a few dashes of silver paint. Clawesome! He's good at seeing how to make something shine.

Together, the two monsters are creating a totally unique show.

"I think Clawdeen is going to be impressed," Barker tells his sister as he steps back to look at their work.

"I hope so," Pawla responds. She sews some bog weeds to the bottom of a swamp-monster skirt.

"It doesn't even matter, though," Barker continues. "The most important thing is that we're friends again. I forgot how much fun it was to fang out."

"Yeah!" agrees Pawla. "It wasn't fun when we were competing. I kept missing my family."

"Even the werepups?" Barker jokes.

Pawla laughs. "*Especially* the werepups. They know how to have a good time!"

The siblings chuckle as they watch their little brothers race around the room trailing ribbons and cobwebs.

The little-sibling styles are finished in no time!

Pawla pulls out her iCoffin and sends a message to her friends: *Monster models, make your way to the art room! It's time for your fright fitting!*

Soon little mansters and ghouls crowd into the art room. They *ooh* and *aah* as they look at the Wolfs' creeptastic creations.

"There is an outfit made especially for each model!" explains Pawla as she shows Alivia her light-up skirt and shirt.

"Voltageous!" exclaims Alivia as she zips up her skirt. "It fits perfectly, and I love these lightning-bolt patterns." She spins around and the electric lights blink purple, red, blue, and green.

"Gore-geous!" Kelpie says as she watches. "Good job, Pawla."

Pawla blushes. "It wasn't just me. Barker helped me with everything. He added the lights."

Barker is helping Pharrah straighten her

crown. He hands her a sarcophagus-shaped purse and she nods approvingly.

"I had one just like this back in my pyramid." She lifts a hand to her head. "Let's see if the crown fits. Give me that mirror?" she instructs Barker imperiously.

He gives the royal mummy a hand mirror and she inspects her reflection.

"This is really golden," she declares. "I love it!"

"Really?" Barker claps in delight.

"Yeah." Pharrah nods, smoothing out the gold pleats of her dress. "You've done amazing work."

"It wasn't just me," Barker tells Pharrah immediately. "Pawla designed all the outfits. The little-sister fashion show was her idea."

Kelpie twirls her scuba skirt. Alivia is

having fun lighting up different colors on her dress.

"I think the show is going to be a big success," Pawla whispers to Barker.

"Totally," Barker agrees.

Pawla hugs her brother. "It was so much fun, but only because we were working as a team. I couldn't have done it without you!"

## CHAPTER 18

# Glitz, Ghouls, and Glamour!

"I was right!" exclaims Mrs. Wolf as she looks around at the art show. "Monster High students are especially creative."

Everybody has contributed something to the art show. The whole school is buzzing with monsters going from project to project.

"Wow!" Dracula examines Lagoona's watercolor display and is impressed. "What a remarkable underwater scene. You have a great sense of color, Lagoona."

"Thanks, Mr. Dracula!" Lagoona responds. "But you should see my little sister Kelpie's artwork. Barker suggested Pawla use it as a pattern for one of the fashion show skirts."

"That's exciting!" says Dracula. "I can't wait to see what the little sisters and brothers have created."

"Me too!" agrees Lagoona.

Mrs. Wolf steps into a darkened corner of the room to see Frankie's glow-in-the-dark paintings. They cover all the walls. "Absolutely electrifying," she announces. "These should be hung in the castle corridors. It would be a creative way of providing light."

"That's a great idea." Frankie smiles. She's happy with how her project turned out. "But the *really* amazing project is the one my sister, Alivia, completed. She took a bunch of photographs and the little-sister fashion show is using them as a backdrop."

"It seems like the little monsters have cooked up something creative!" says Mrs. Wolf.

"Speaking of which," Clawdeen says beside her, "I think the little-sister show is about to start."

Everyone crowds into the Creepeteria. Fangelica has made cookies in the shapes of hats, boots, sunglasses, and bow ties. Gob tries to swallow the whole tray, but she pulls them away just in time. The tables and coffin chairs have been cleared away to make room for a runway. The lights are dimmed and Alivia activates a sparkling disco ball.

*"Oohh!"* Frankie cries. "What a great touch! Of course my sister would think of cool lighting."

Alivia's photographs are projected onto a screen and the music starts! Rayth, Deuce, and Skelly have teamed up with Ari Hauntington to sing a style-themed song. They start to rock out as the little sister models stream down the runway.

Kelpie is dazzling. Her skirt flows across the runway like river water. She wears long seashell earrings and seaweed-strap sandals.

Alivia stops to twirl, and all her lights blink. At the last minute, Barker gave her some bolt-and-nail rings to wear on her fingers. Pawla was sure to glue metallic hearts onto Alivia's tights.

"I want some of those!" exclaims Frankie.

"I'd wear them so much they'd be my everyday uniform."

"Every*night* uniform," Draculaura corrects her friend, smiling. "I agree. But what I really want are those polka-dot-printed vampire V-necks. They are scary cute."

Fangelica is modeling her built-in-apron dress. She reaches into a pocket, pulls out confetti, and throws it over the crowd.

"Yum!" Some of the confetti lands on Mrs. Wolf's tongue. "Edible confetti! I wonder who thought of that!"

It was Barker's idea, but Pawla and Fangelica helped him create the sugary flakes.

Each outfit is a success. The crowd claps and the models come back to show off their werecatwalks.

"These styles are boo-tiful and surprising!" Mrs. Wolf decides as she claps. "It looks like the littlest monsters have a lot to teach us about creative teamwork."

Finally, Barker and Pawla walk down the runway wearing matching graphic T-shirts. On each shirt is a picture of a wolf howling at the full moon.

"I'll take a couple of those!" Clawdeen calls out.

The whole room erupts in applause as the weresiblings take a bow. All the little-monster models come out and hug Pawla and Barker.

"You're the beast!" Pawla tells her brother as the show finishes. "I mean—the best!"

"Best beast? I'll take it!" jokes Barker. "I think you're the best beast too, sis."

"This is a total monster success," Clawdeen says to her little brother and sister.

"Yeah?" Pawla asks. "I was so inspired by your show."

"Yours is even better," Clawdeen tells her little sister. "These designs are beyond clawesome. I'm so proud of you guys. My siblings are the most stylish Monster High students."

From a distance, Mrs. Wolf watches as her werechildren do a group hug.

"I think I can safely say," she comments to Dracula, "the little monster brothers and sisters stole the show!"